This book belongs to:

....

For Mia, Talulla, and Ronin

About this book

I wrote this book for my granddaughter Talulla who, like many children, sometimes finds it difficult to fall asleep. In my experience, children often resist a direct order to "go to sleep"—such a demand may actually make them more alert and awake. They respond more comfortably to indirect suggestion and an invitation to explore relaxation.

When I had trouble falling asleep myself, I explored different ways to relax, feel safe in my world, and let the sleep drift in. I grew up in the noise of America's urban east coast, then moved to the quiet pinion-scented mountains of New Mexico. Now when I move back and forth between busy cities and the deep quiet of wild spaces, I find it helpful to remember that safe, spacious, connected quiet of the wild world. I take that peacefulness with me when I head to New York or London and remember it when I drift off at night. I know how relaxing it is to feel connected to the rhythms of nature, even if the only way to feel it is in your mind's eye. It's this I share with you here.

This sleepytime tale is best read when your little one is all ready for bed and tucked in cozily, or at anytime to calm a restless child. By joining Talulla Bear on her meditative journey, I hope your child will find that deep place of rest and peace, a place where all is right with the world, and sleep is just a step over a gentle doorway …

TALULLA BEAR'S
BEDTIME BOOK

A Sleepytime Tale...

HEATHER ROAN ROBBINS

Illustrations by Sarah Perkins

CICO kidz

I'm not sleepy ...

Are you all ready for bed?
All clean and shiny?
Have you done those things that help your
body rest and be ready for tomorrow?

Yes, but I still can't sleep.
Okay, little one, then let's enjoy the
quiet gift of the night.

Look, the cat is going to sleep.
How can you tell?
She's stretching her body, relaxing all her
muscles, tired from a busy day.

She makes her body so long as she stretches
her front paws way above her head, and her
back paws stretch way below.

Can you stretch like a cat? Can you
stretch your front paws way above your head,
and reach your back paws way below?
Can you make your body as long as the cat?

Well done, little bear.
Now she's curling up, as soft and
loose as a fur puddle.
How would you lie as soft and loose
as a fur puddle?
My good little bear.

Listen, the dog is asleep.
How can you tell?
You can hear how slowly he's breathing.

We can count with him.
He breathes in 1, 2, 3
and out 1, 2, 3. So slowly.
Can you breathe as slow as the dog?
In 1, 2, 3, out 1, 2, 3.

Let's breathe like the dog.
The sleeping dog.

If the cat and dog are sleeping all soft
and cozy, all floppy and relaxed,
we know the house is safe and quiet.

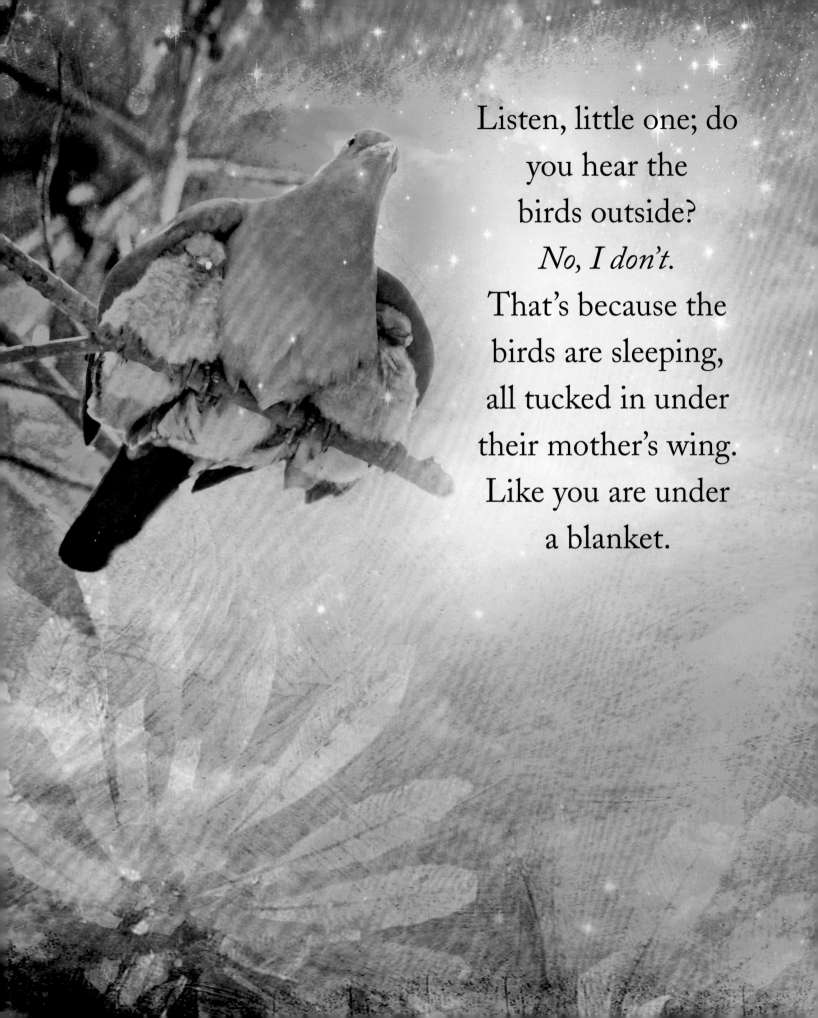

Listen, little one; do
you hear the
birds outside?
No, I don't.
That's because the
birds are sleeping,
all tucked in under
their mother's wing.
Like you are under
a blanket.

I wrap this blanket around you
like the wing of a mommy bird.
All safe. All cozy.

Can you imagine yourself as
a baby bird, all safe and cozy?
Do you feel a warm, soft wing
wrapped around you?

The birds are nested in the trees.
Trees love the night.

As the trees rest, they grow slowly and gently,
reaching their roots way down into the ground,
growing strong, safe, and secure.
Strong enough to hold the birds, bees, and bears
and give them a safe place to rest.
As the wind blows gently through their leaves,
the air feeds the trees and the trees refresh the air.

Can you imagine being under a big, wide,
strong tree, little bear?

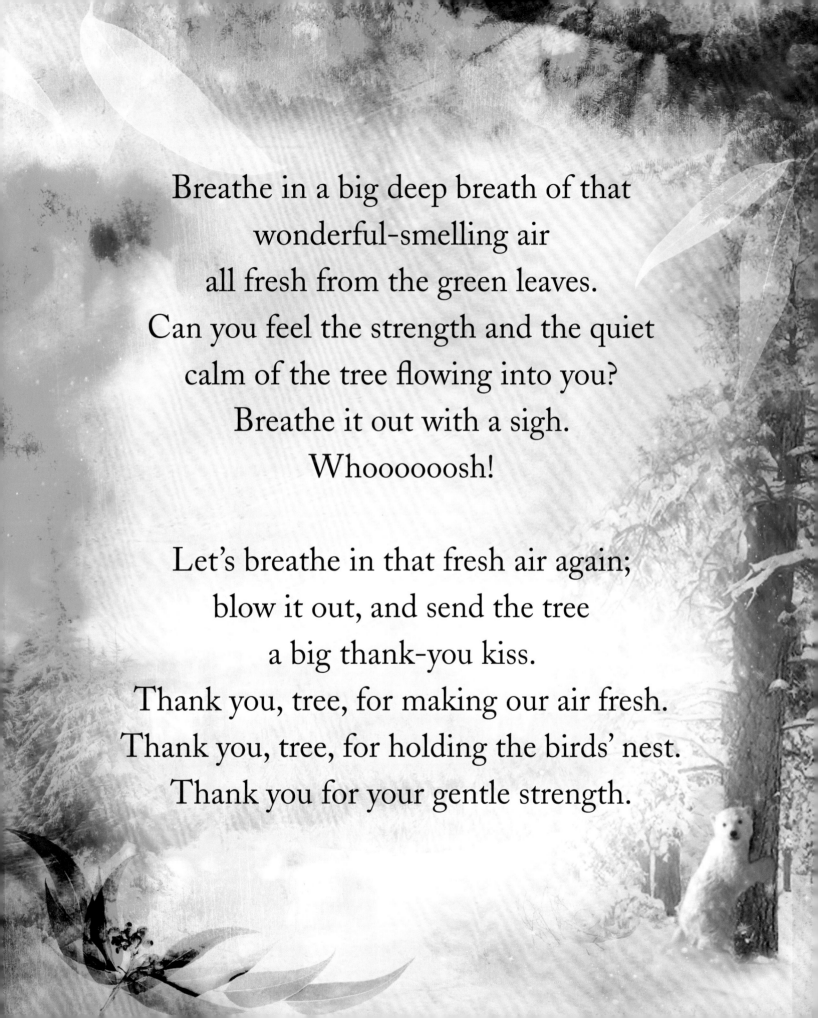

Breathe in a big deep breath of that
wonderful-smelling air
all fresh from the green leaves.
Can you feel the strength and the quiet
calm of the tree flowing into you?
Breathe it out with a sigh.
Whoooooosh!

Let's breathe in that fresh air again;
blow it out, and send the tree
a big thank-you kiss.
Thank you, tree, for making our air fresh.
Thank you, tree, for holding the birds' nest.
Thank you for your gentle strength.

And behind the tree, when the fluffy
clouds slowly drift apart,
what twinkles in the night sky, little bear?
The moon and the stars.

Yes, the stars twinkle in the night sky, shining down
on us as they have since the beginning of time.
Beautiful stars sprinkled like jewels, more
than we could ever count. But it's fun to try…
we can let our mind's eye run over them and count,

1, 2, 3, 4 …

How many can you count?

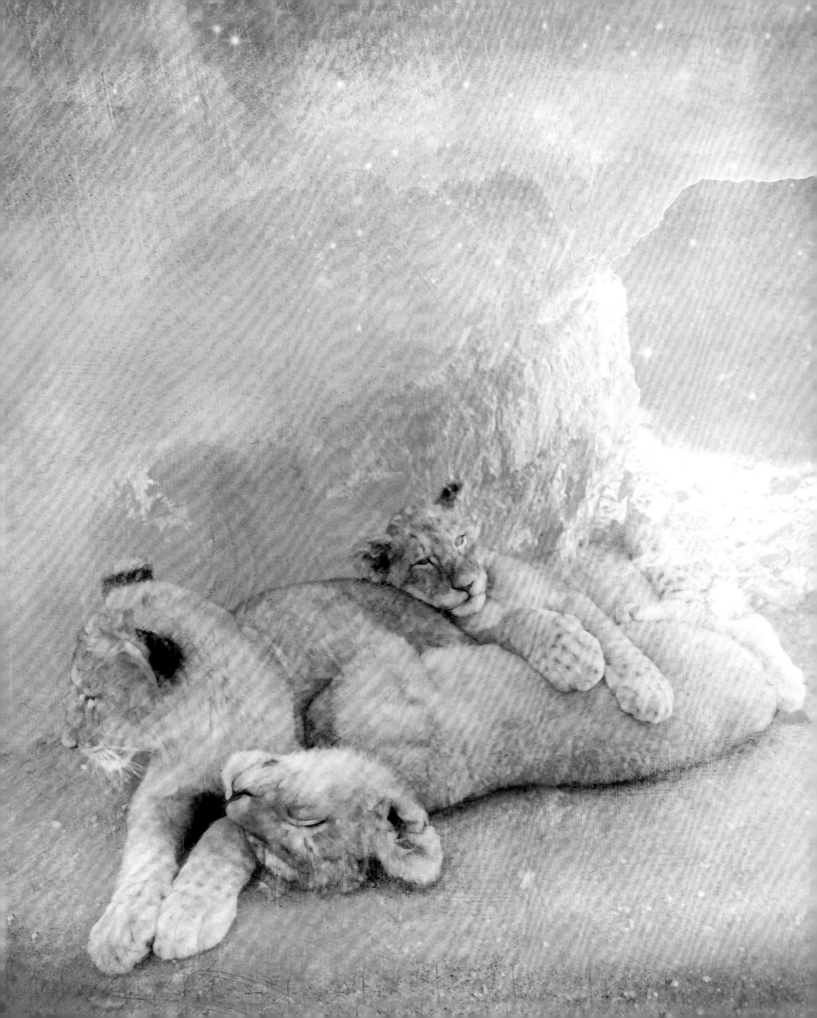

Those same stars shine down
on animals whose eyes have
grown heavy after a long day.
Their eyes drift closed to rest,
safe in their nests and burrows
all around the world.

And the stars shine down on sleeping children,
resting deeply, dreaming gently,
sleeping soundly all around.

Sleep well ... Sweet dreams ...
Shine on, stars.

Breathe gently, trees; be cozy, baby birds.
Cuddle up, little ones.

Sleep well, Talulla Bear.

You too ...

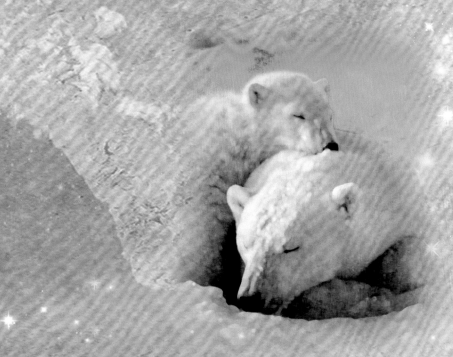

Published in 2016 by CICO Books
An imprint of Ryland Peters & Small Ltd
20–21 Jockey's Fields London WC1R 4BW
341 E 116th St New York, NY 10029

www.rylandpeters.com

10 9 8 7 6 5 4 3 2 1

Text © Heather Roan Robbins 2016
Design and illustrations © CICO Books 2016

A CIP catalog record for this book is available from the Library of
Congress and the British Library.

ISBN: 978-1-78249-379-2

Printed in China

Designer: Emily Breen
In-house editor: Dawn Bates
Art director: Sally Powell
Head of production: Patricia Harrington
Publishing manager: Penny Craig
Publisher: Cindy Richards

Polar Bears International work to ensure polar
bears remain a part of the Arctic forever.
Go to www.polarbearsinternational.org